The Gingham Dog *and the* Calico Cat

Season of Harmony

By Brigid Clark and Chris Noel
Illustrated by Laszlo Kubinyi

RH /Rabbit Ears
NEW YORK

Published in the United States by Random House, Inc., New York.
ISBN: 0-679-81573-2 (hardcover); 0-679-81575-9 (paperback)
Manufactured in the United States of America   10 9 8 7 6 5 4 3 2 1

If you'd been standing in your backyard on a starry Christmas Eve not long ago, and if you'd been listening very carefully indeed, you might've heard Santa's sleighbells coming — and you'd have jumped for joy! But then you'd have stopped, not believing your ears.... *What was that?* For it was on that night, not long ago, that the Calico Cat and the Gingham Dog filled the heavens with the sounds of their fighting. And that was the Christmas Eve when the Calico Cat and the Gingham Dog fell out of Santa's sleigh and found harmony in their new home.

Now, as you may have heard, the Gingham Dog and the Calico Cat were enemies from the very moment they were made. You see, they were made in anger by two elves who were acting very foolishly toward each other, and who wanted to see who could make the best toy in Santa's whole workshop.

They cut cloth and they sewed cloth and they stuffed their animals with cotton batting and their hands moved so quickly that they looked like a hundred hands to the other elves who had gathered round to watch. While they worked, the two elves said terrible things to each other, like:

"I'll bet your toy will have its ears on backwards!" and "Well, you'll probably forget to put the ears on in the first place, to say nothing of the tail!"

When they had finished, the two elves proudly placed their toys onto the wooden workshop table to compare them. The one elf had made a white puppy with floppy, furry ears and a gingham bow around his neck. The other elf had made a caramel, black, and white kitty with long, silky whiskers and a calico bow around her neck.

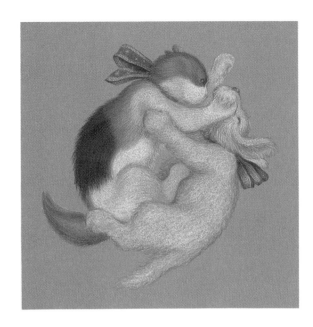

Then, to the astonishment of all the elves, the Gingham Dog and the Calico Cat opened their eyes, stood up, and leapt at each other, tumbling in a furious ball of arms and legs. At that moment, Santa stepped into the workshop, tugging at his long white beard, and said:

"Toys, toys. You're breaking my heart. Elves, don't you understand what you have done? You both became so angry with one another that you forgot to make your toys out of love."

The two elves stared down at their feet.

"You put so much bad feeling into making these toys that they came to life with anger inside them."

The elves looked up at Santa and nodded sadly.

"It will take a powerful love to change them now," Santa said, "a powerful love indeed."

And then he sighed and shook his head.

And so it was. Even on Christmas Eve the two animals
continued to fight, pushing and snapping at each other atop
the very largest bag on Santa's sleigh.

Then suddenly, without warning, a great wind came and blew the two bickering animals right off the sleigh and into the cold empty night.

"Help!" they cried. "Santa! Help!"

But Santa only gazed down at them lovingly.

"Do not be afraid," he called to them. "If you will only help each other from now on, you will find your way home! Goodbye, my little friends — and good luck!"

And even before they had time to be afraid, they landed — *whump, thump* — in the middle of a snowdrift at the very center of a great big forest.

"Ouch! My nose is flattened!" cried Calico Cat, sticking her head above the snow.

"Ick! My ears got crimped!" whined Gingham Dog, as his head popped up beside hers.

They climbed out of the drift and shook themselves free of powdery snow. Then they looked slowly around at the dark, unfriendly trees and the strange blinking eyes of the forest's night creatures all around them. And then they began to cry. They cried for a long while before they realized that it was far too cold to stand apart, so they snuggled up together and felt much warmer.

"What are we going to do?" cried Gingham Dog.

"Oh, I don't know! It's so cold and dark here."

Unable to sit still, Gingham Dog stood up and looked about, blinking his tears away.

"Well, we might as well start walking—unless you're too much of a scaredy cat!"

But this made Calico Cat cry even harder.

"Oh, I'm sorry," said Gingham Dog, and he took her paws in his and helped her up. "Being scared makes me talk without thinking."

"Me too!" said Calico Cat.

Together they set out along a little pathway into the unknown darkness.

Gingham Dog sighed. "Christmas Eve is supposed to be the happiest night of our lives, when Santa puts us inside a warm, cozy home under the tree so the children will find us and love us."

"But here we are," said Calico Cat. "All alone, in the middle of nowhere, and—gracious, what's that?"

She pointed off through the trees. Far in the distance there was a clearing, and in this clearing they could see a small building. A lamp shone through a window, brightening the snow.

"It must be some kind of workshop!" cried Gingham Dog.

They could hardly believe their eyes! They jumped up and down and danced in each other's furry little arms. Then they began running toward it, but they couldn't go very fast, for the snow was deep. They didn't know if they would make it to the lighted window, still so far away. But they had to, they simply had to…

Now, although they didn't know it, what they were struggling toward was not a workshop but a cottage—a snug and welcoming cottage, and inside it was a mother, a father, a girl named Jessica, her little brother named Owen, and their grandmother. The whole family was gathered around the dinner table, and Jessica and Owen were so excited they could scarcely keep their seats.

"Grandma," asked Jessica, "when do you think Santa will come?"

"Will we be awake?" Owen asked.

"Oh, children. You know perfectly well that Saint Nicholas only comes when everyone is asleep! Even old women like me don't know just when!"

"Well, I'm going to stay up! I'm going to catch him!" cried Owen, banging his fork on the dinner table.

Mother and Father and Grandmother laughed, but Jessica didn't think he was so funny.

"Oh no, you won't! You can't catch Santa! Nobody can! He's a miracle!" she said.

"I can if I want! I can too!" Owen hollered.

"You're only a little boy! Isn't he, Mama? Just a little boy!"

"Now, Jessica," said Mother, "there's no need to quarrel!"

"You two fight like cats and dogs!" said Father. "And on Christmas Eve!"

Later, after dinner, Jessica stood at the window, thinking about her Christmas wish. More than anything in the world, she wished for something all her own—but not just anything. It had to be a wonderful thing that was hers alone. Mother and Father always made her share everything with her brother. Sometimes, when she was playing outside, Jessica would lift up a great armful of snow and hug it, pretending it was this special something all her own.

But she knew perfectly well that if she tried to take it inside, the wind would blow most of it away and then, once she *was* inside, the rest of it would only melt.

Pressing her nose to the chilly glass, it seemed to Jessica that all her best dreams in the world were like that—not solid, not lasting... And as she looked up at the sky she saw that clouds had covered the stars and it was beginning to snow.

Meanwhile, back in the wintry forest, the Calico Cat and the Gingham Dog found themselves in quite a predicament. They had arrived at the edge of a brook, not at all sure how to cross it. The light from the cottage twinkled at them up ahead, urging them onward.

❄
_____

"Oh, if we don't make it across this stream, I don't know what will happen!" said Calico Cat. "It's so terribly cold—and look, it's starting to snow!"

"Remember what Santa told us," said Gingham Dog. "He told us to help each other. We have to work together...Hmm... Let me think a minute..."

He sat down and thumped his tail on the snow.

"Excuse me, Gingham—"

"Hush now, Calico—"

"But—"

"How can I think if you're chattering at me?" said Gingham Dog.

"But I think I have an answer! Let's push that big tree branch off that rock. I think when it falls it will make a nice bridge for us!"

"What an excellent idea!" cried Gingham Dog.

And together they pushed and shoved and squeaked and puffed, and at last the giant tree branch fell into place, and the two of them crossed over just as neatly as you please, paw in paw. But the snow was even deeper on the other side of the brook! And the flakes were falling more heavily every minute!

＊
_____

Back inside the cottage, Jessica and Owen were just being tucked into bed.

"There," said Father, pulling the blankets up to Owen's chin. "The sooner you fall asleep, the sooner it'll be Christmas!"

Mother and Father and Grandma kissed the two children, and then left the room. "Good night."

"I'll bet I can get to sleep before you," said Owen.

"Well, I'm already asleep, so there!" said Jessica.

"No, you're not!"

"Oh yes, I am! I'm talking in my sleep!"

Owen decided not to answer his sister. Instead, he just lay there thinking about his Christmas wish. In a quiet, quiet whisper that no one else could hear except Santa, Owen asked for a pet. He would take any kind of pet, but a little kitten, or a puppy, that would be perfect—*perfect*—something he could hold and cuddle for as long as he wanted, that *no one* would make him let go of…Then Owen fell asleep, dreaming that his wish had come true.

Suddenly Owen awoke. He thought he'd heard a sound outside. Maybe it was Santa! Maybe he could *see* Santa! He slipped out from between the covers and very quietly made his way to the door.

"Hey, what are you doing up?" Jessica said when she saw her brother standing frozen in the middle of a giant step. "You can't go downstairs! It's not morning yet!"

"I thought I heard Santa!" Owen replied, and he disappeared into the dark hallway.

"But you can't! You'll scare him away! You'll ruin everything!"

And in a moment, she too was out of bed and racing after her brother down the stairs.

Owen grabbed the lamp from the kitchen and went straight to the front door. Jessica was right behind him, but by the time she got there Owen was already halfway outside.

"I'm going to see Santa!"

As Owen was saying this, much to her surprise Jessica thought she saw something moving at the edge of the clearing. She peered harder, trying to see through the falling snow.

"Over there!" she said, pointing. "Owen, shine the lamp over there!"

"Th-th-that must be a child," shivered the Calico Cat in a very weak voice, her teeth chattering.

"T-t-two children," said the Gingham Dog.

"It's just like Santa said!"

The two poor creatures looked at each other, ice and snow clinging to their whiskers.

"Do you think this could be our home?" asked Gingham Dog.

"Oh, I do, I do," said Calico Cat hopefully. "I believe they're coming for us!"

It was true. Owen and Jessica, wearing only their pajamas and slippers, were racing across the snow-covered yard toward the edge of the clearing.

The Calico Cat and the Gingham Dog stood up and started brushing the snow off each other. But in no time the two children were upon them. Owen swept the Calico Cat into his arms, and Jessica picked up the Gingham Dog and hugged him to her chest. He was just as soft as the snow she'd hugged before—and he wouldn't blow away or melt!

Here, *here* was her Christmas wish, something she could keep all to herself.

Everyone was so excited that they forgot all about how cold their feet were.

And Owen was busy thinking: *Santa heard me! Santa heard me! Now I never have to let go of my very own pet!*

The Calico Cat and the Gingham Dog, each squeezed in the arms of a loving child, called out to each other.

"I was just about to give up," Gingham Dog admitted.

"Me too!" said Calico Cat.

"Listen to that!" said Jessica. "They're meowing and barking to each other!"

"And you know what?" said the Gingham Dog. "I'm so glad we'll be together from now on!"

"Me too!"

They jumped down out of the children's arms and ran, side by side, through the snow toward the cottage. Jessica and Owen looked at each other and laughed. Then they ran to catch up.

They were all safely inside when Grandma came downstairs. "What have we here?" she asked.

But Jessica and Owen could only sit on the sofa and point in delight to the cat and the dog jumping and dashing about on the living room carpet. Grandma sat down with them. She too was amazed.

Around and around in a circle the animals ran, first the cat chasing the dog, then the dog chasing the cat. They seemed to be playing tag.

Oh, how wonderful! Owen and Jessica and Grandma laughed. And they laughed even harder when the animals began to wrestle and tumble around the room together! Watching them, Jessica saw that the two animals loved each other very much and she knew it would be wrong to keep the dog all to herself, apart from his dear friend.

And Owen thought to himself: *Well, I didn't get a pet... I got two of them...And so did Jessica!*

❄
_____

Before he knew it, his sister had jumped on top of him and they too wrestled and tumbled together, giggling.

This time, it was the animals' turn to watch in delight. And as they stood leaning against each other, they could feel the warmth of their new home curl up around them and melt the last of the ice and snow from their whiskers.

"Well!" said Grandma. "It sure will take us a long time to fall asleep this Christmas Eve—but something tells me Saint Nick won't mind!"

"I'd say he's been here already," said Father.

Jessica and Owen turned to each other and smiled.

And so it was, one Christmas Eve not so very long ago, that
the Calico Cat and the Gingham Dog fell from Santa's sleigh
and found harmony and love in their new home.